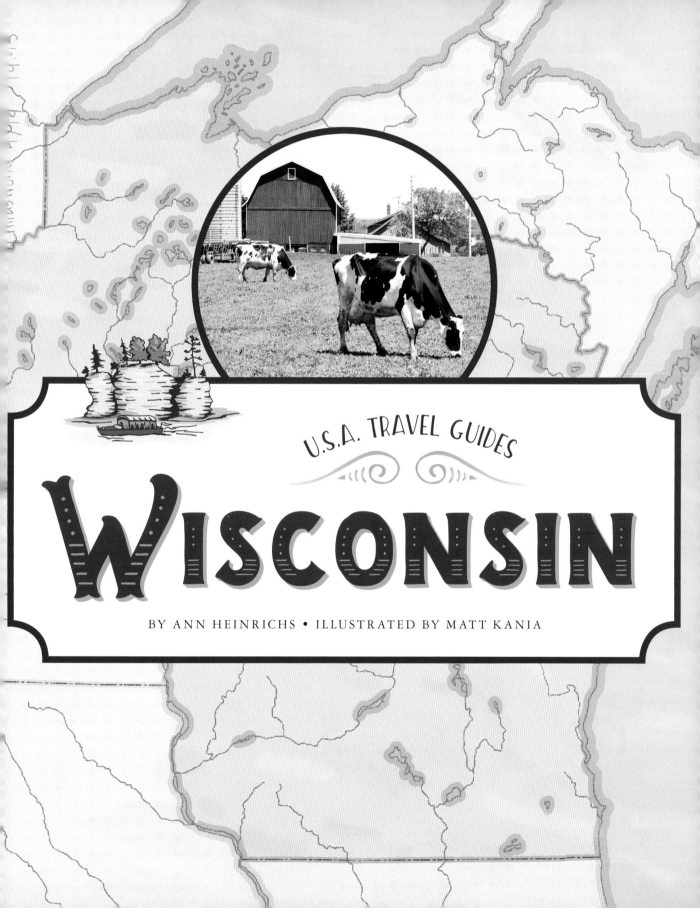

U.S.A. TRAVEL GUIDES

WISCONSIN

BY ANN HEINRICHS • ILLUSTRATED BY MATT KANIA

The Child's World®
childsworld.com

Published by The Child's World®
1980 Lookout Drive • Mankato, MN 56003-1705
800-599-READ • www.childsworld.com

Photo Credits

Copyright

ISBN 9781503819894
LCCN 2016961201

Printing

Printed in the United States of America
PA02334

Ann Heinrichs is the author of more than 100 books for children and young adults. She has also enjoyed successful careers as a children's book editor and an advertising copywriter. Ann grew up in Fort Smith, Arkansas, and lives in Chicago, Illinois.

About the Author
Ann Heinrichs

Matt Kania loves maps and, as a kid, dreamed of making them. In school he studied geography and cartography, and today he makes maps for a living. Matt's favorite thing about drawing maps is learning about the places they represent. Many of the maps he has created can be found in books, magazines, videos, Web sites, and public places.

About the
Map Illustrator
Matt Kania

*On the cover: Keep an eye out for dairy
cows when you travel in Wisconsin.*

OUR WISCONSIN TRIP

WISCONSIN

Ready for a tour of the Badger State? You're in for a great ride. You'll meet **lumberjacks** and Cheeseheads. You'll learn about bison and see a leaping dog. You'll race a snowmobile and milk a cow. You'll even get the scoop on those badgers! So buckle up and follow that dotted line. Away we go!

WELCOME TO WISCONSIN

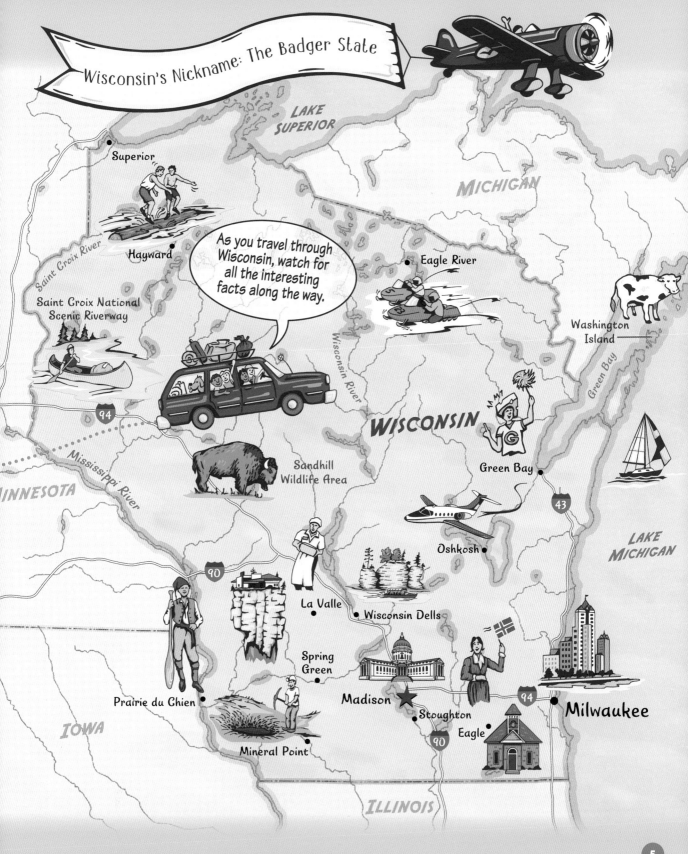

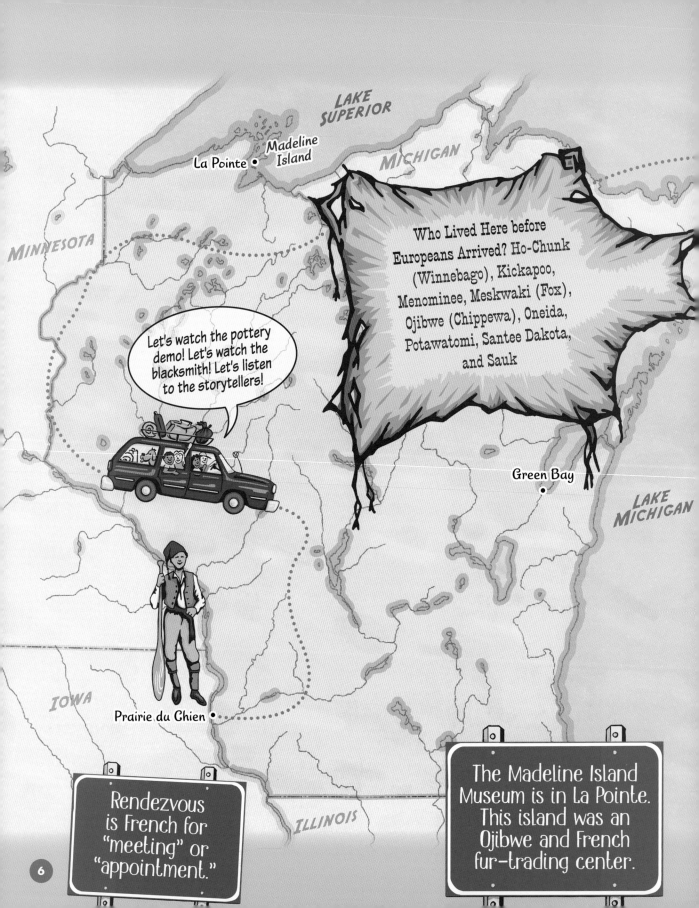

PRAIRIE DU CHIEN'S PRAIRIE VILLA RENDEZVOUS

Clang! The blacksmith hammers red-hot metal. Chunk! The **tomahawk** chops into a stump. You're at the Prairie Villa Rendezvous! Prairie du Chien holds this event every year. It celebrates life in Wisconsin's early days.

Frenchmen were the first Europeans in Wisconsin. Jean Nicolet was the first to arrive. He was a French explorer from Canada. Nicolet arrived in Green Bay in 1634. He claimed Wisconsin for France. Soon other Frenchmen arrived. They traded with Native Americans including the Ho-Chunk and Oneida peoples for furs.

Prairie du Chien was a fur-trading post in the 1700s. Native Americans and French traders met there to exchange goods.

Jean Nicolet was the first European known to have reached what is now Wisconsin.

BADGER HOLES IN MINERAL POINT

Roam the hills around Pendarvis. You'll see big holes here and there. What are those holes all about?

Pendarvis is an old miners' village in Mineral Point. Lead was discovered there in the 1820s. Thousands of **immigrants** came in to work the mines.

At first, the miners had no houses. They lived in holes they dug in the hillsides. People called these shelters badger holes. That's why Wisconsin is called the Badger State!

See how miners lived in the Pendarvis house.

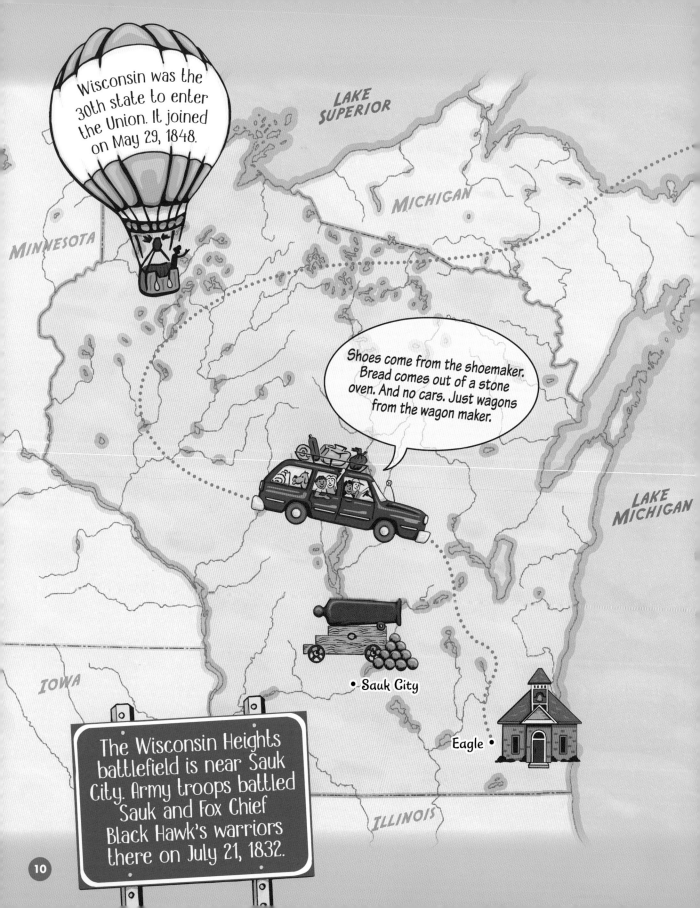

There's a woman wearing a long dress. She's cooking over an open fire. Beyond the log cabin, a man is plowing. Horses pull his wooden plow. What are these folks up to? Just ask!

You're at Old World Wisconsin near Eagle. It's like an 1800s immigrant village. People in historic clothing are busy at their chores. They'll tell you exactly what they're up to!

People from many lands moved into Wisconsin. Some came from Denmark, Finland, or Norway. Others came from Germany, Poland, Ireland, or Wales. African Americans who had been enslaved in the South came, too. Everyone worked hard to make new homes.

Visit a 1906 schoolhouse at Old World Wisconsin.

Draw an ugly **troll**. Make it look really mean and snarling. Maybe you'll win the ugly-troll-drawing contest! It's part of Syttende Mai. That's a big Norwegian festival in Stoughton.

Wisconsin's **ethnic** groups hold lots of fun festivals. For Germans, it's Oktoberfest. Czechs hold Cesky Den. The Chinese celebrate the Moon Festival. Polish, Italian, Mexican, French, Native American—you name it! They all share their food, music, and fun.

Sometimes people make long bratwursts at Oktoberfest.

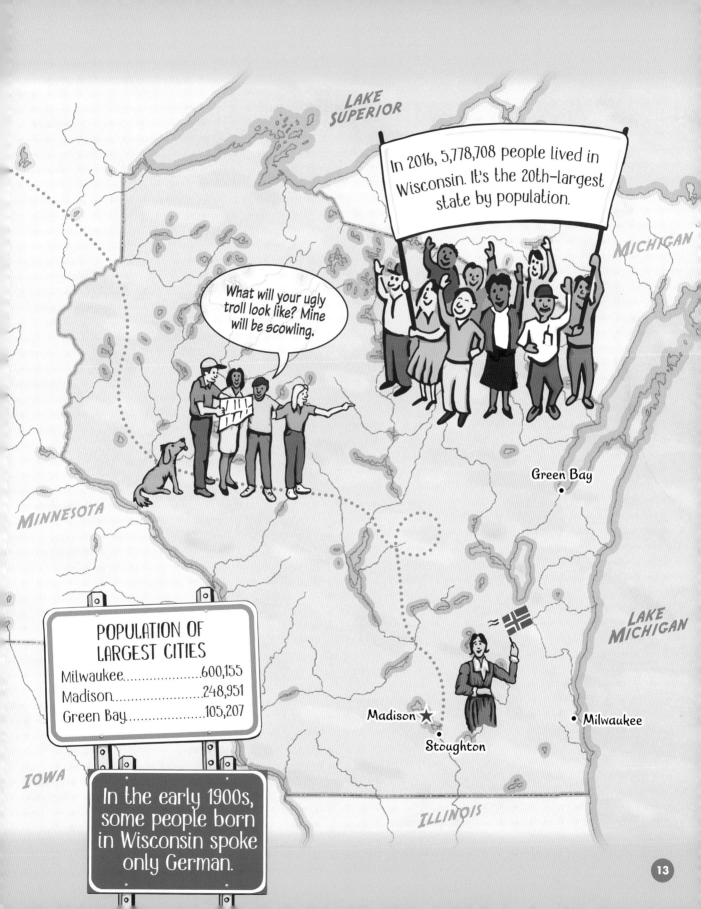

In 2016, 5,778,708 people lived in Wisconsin. It's the 20th-largest state by population.

What will your ugly troll look like? Mine will be scowling.

POPULATION OF LARGEST CITIES
Milwaukee.....................600,155
Madison.......................248,951
Green Bay.....................105,207

In the early 1900s, some people born in Wisconsin spoke only German.

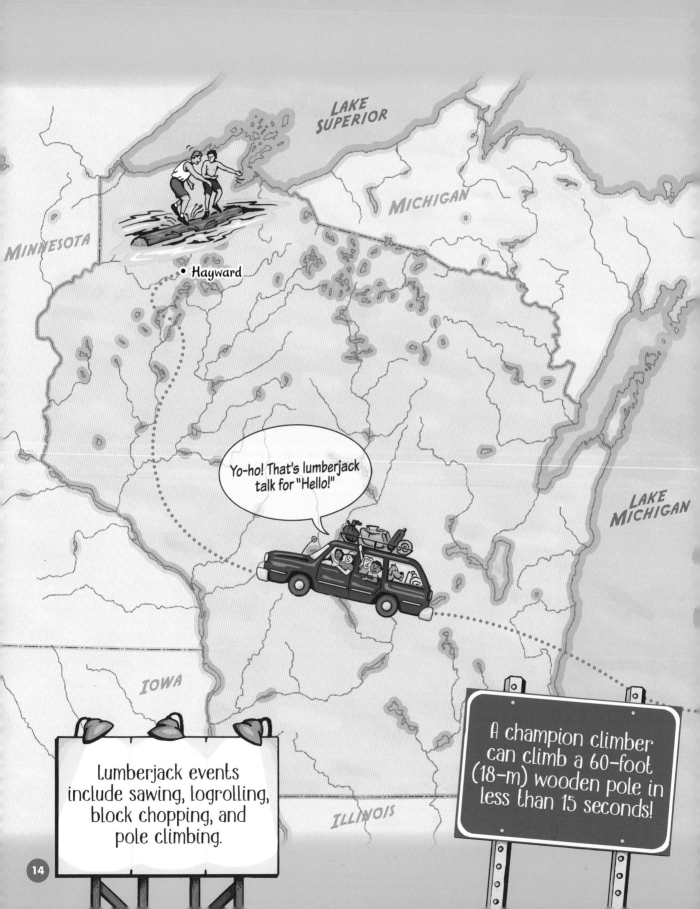

LAKE SUPERIOR

MICHIGAN

MINNESOTA

• Hayward

Yo-ho! That's lumberjack talk for "Hello!"

LAKE MICHIGAN

IOWA

ILLINOIS

Lumberjack events include sawing, logrolling, block chopping, and pole climbing.

A champion climber can climb a 60-foot (18-m) wooden pole in less than 15 seconds!

THE LUMBERJACK WORLD CHAMPIONSHIPS IN HAYWARD

Look around. Sawdust and wood chips are flying. People are wobbling on logs in the water. Oops—somebody fell in!

You're at the Lumberjack World Championships in Hayward. It celebrates Wisconsin's logging days. Logging was a big **industry** in the late 1800s.

Dense forests once covered northern Wisconsin. Lumberjacks cut the trees down. They floated the logs down the rivers. The logs went to sawmills and paper mills.

By the way, lumberjacking is not an all-male sport. Women and girls compete, too. They're called lumberjills!

Wood chips fly as lumberjacks chop logs in record time.

Hundreds of musicians. Jillions of food stands. It's Summerfest time in Milwaukee!

Almost 900,000 people visit Milwaukee for Summerfest. But Milwaukee works as hard as it plays. It's booming with business and industry.

Many immigrants settled in Milwaukee. They helped the city grow. They worked in flour mills and meat plants. German people opened beer **breweries**. Ships and railroads shipped their goods out. Milwaukee became a center for both manufacturing and banking. Now it's the biggest city in Wisconsin.

Get a bird's-eye view of Summerfest!

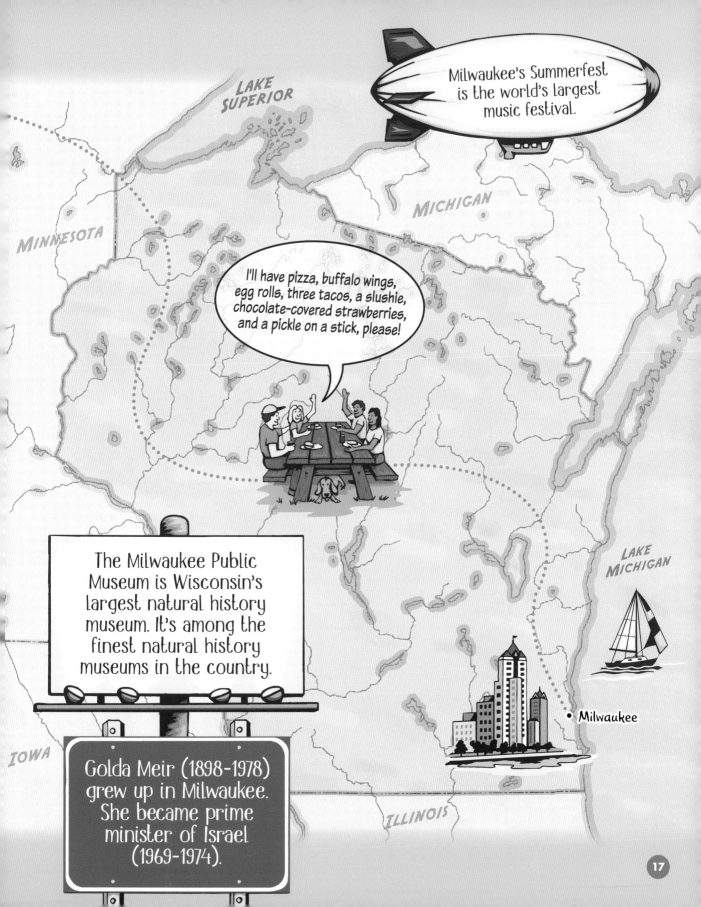

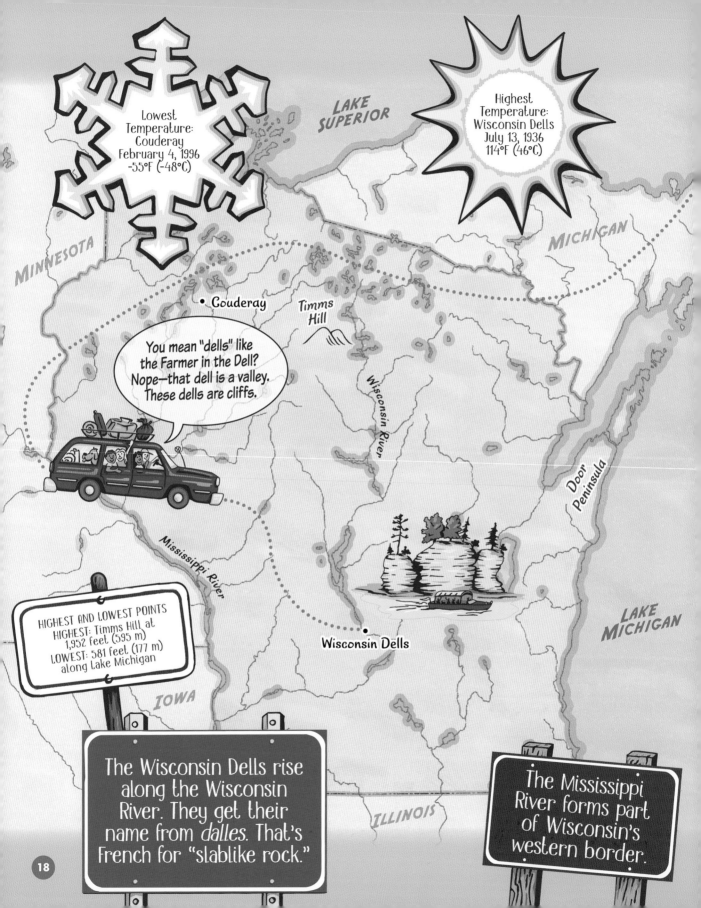

LAKE SUPERIOR

Lowest Temperature: Couderay February 4, 1996 -55°F (-48°C)

Highest Temperature: Wisconsin Dells July 13, 1936 114°F (46°C)

MINNESOTA

MICHIGAN

• Couderay

Timms Hill

Wisconsin River

You mean "dells" like the Farmer in the Dell? Nope—that dell is a valley. These dells are cliffs.

Door Peninsula

Mississippi River

LAKE MICHIGAN

HIGHEST AND LOWEST POINTS
HIGHEST: Timms Hill at 1,952 feet (595 m)
LOWEST: 581 feet (177 m) along Lake Michigan

Wisconsin Dells

IOWA

The Wisconsin Dells rise along the Wisconsin River. They get their name from *dalles*. That's French for "slablike rock."

ILLINOIS

The Mississippi River forms part of Wisconsin's western border.

WISCONSIN DELLS AND THE LEAPING DOG

He crouches. He springs. He sails through mid-air. Good doggie! This is no circus—it's the Wisconsin Dells. Rushing waters carved its towering rock formations. You'll see the dog at Stand Rock. He leaps across to it from a high cliff. Give that dog a treat!

The Dells are in south-central Wisconsin. High cliffs rise in the southwest, too. Rolling plains cover much of central Wisconsin. The north is hilly with many little lakes.

Wisconsin borders two of the Great Lakes. Lake Superior is on the north. Lake Michigan is on the southeast. Now, think of Wisconsin as a mitten. The Door **Peninsula** would be its thumb!

Make a splash at one of Wisconsin Dells' many water parks.

THE SNOWMOBILE DERBY IN EAGLE RIVER

Dashing through the snow. In a what? A Ski-doo and an Arctic Cat? No one-horse open sleighs here. You're at the Track Snowmobile Derby in Eagle River. Why not join the racers? There's a division for kids, too.

Wisconsin is a great place for winter sports. You can ski, ice-skate, and snowmobile. And sleigh rides? You can get those, too!

For summer fun, there's hiking, biking, and fishing. The Door Peninsula is popular for camping. Wisconsin Dells offers boat rides and water parks. And then there's that leaping dog!

Snowmobiles take off at the beginning of a race in Eagle River.

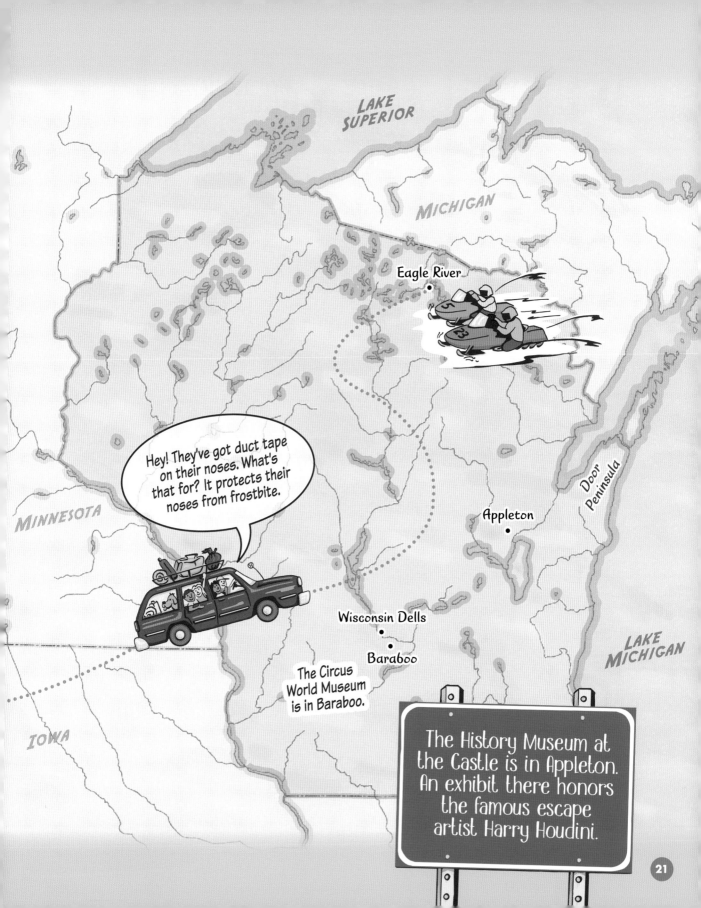

STATE TREE
SUGAR MAPLE

STATE BIRD
ROBIN

STATE FLOWER
WOOD VIOLET

LAKE SUPERIOR

MINNESOTA

MICHIGAN

• Rhinelander

There are approximately 15 bison at Sandhill Wildlife Area.

Sandhill Wildlife Area

LAKE MICHIGAN

In Lakota tradition, a young woman appeared as a white bison 2,000 years ago. She promised she would return to bring world peace.

IOWA

The hodag is Rhinelander's official animal. Hodags are mean and fierce. They have sharp teeth and claws and spikes along their back. But they don't really exist!

ILLINOIS

The National Park Service has four sites in Wisconsin.

SANDHILL WILDLIFE AREA BISON

Drive along Trumpeter Trail. A herd of bison grazes in the distance. Climb the observation tower to get a bird's-eye view. You're at Sandhill Wildlife Area!

Bison used to roam across Wisconsin's plains. But hunters killed off the big herds. Many other animals still live in Wisconsin's woods. The thickest forests are in the north. They're home to deer, bears, foxes, and rabbits. And don't forget the badgers! They still dig holes in the hillsides.

Bison spend much of their day grazing.

The capitol's dome is huge. It's the fourth largest in the world. And underneath that dome are the state government offices. While you're there, keep an eye out for badgers. They're hidden around the building!

Wisconsin's government has three branches. One branch is the **legislature**. It makes state laws. The governor leads another branch. This branch carries out the laws. Courts make up the third branch. Their judges decide whether laws have been broken.

The capitol's dome is 284.4 feet (86.7 m) high.

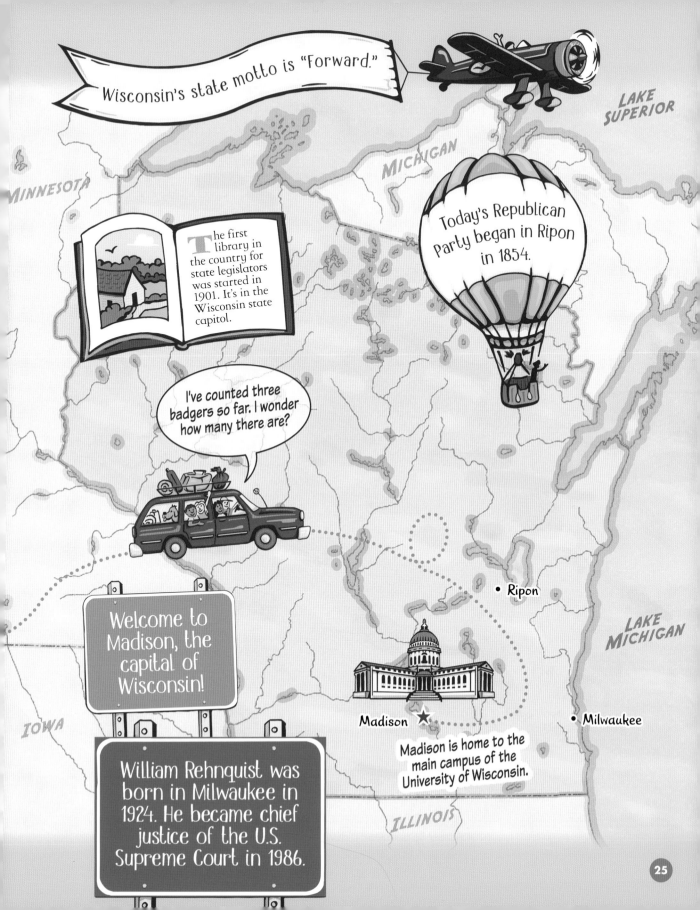

Wisconsin's state motto is "Forward."

The first library in the country for state legislators was started in 1901. It's in the Wisconsin state capitol.

Today's Republican Party began in Ripon in 1854.

I've counted three badgers so far. I wonder how many there are?

Welcome to Madison, the capital of Wisconsin!

William Rehnquist was born in Milwaukee in 1924. He became chief justice of the U.S. Supreme Court in 1986.

Madison is home to the main campus of the University of Wisconsin.

LAKE SUPERIOR

MINNESOTA

MICHIGAN

• Ripon

LAKE MICHIGAN

Madison ★

• Milwaukee

IOWA

ILLINOIS

A FARM VACATION ON WASHINGTON ISLAND

Cluck! Time to feed the chickens! Baa! Give that lamb its bottle! You call this a vacation? Yes! It's a Tipping Bucket Farm vacation. You're on a farm on Washington Island. The guests help with the chores. Vacationers say it's fantastic!

Wisconsin has many farm animals, including thousands of **dairy** cattle. They give tons of milk! Much of that milk becomes butter and cheese. Lots of farmers raise beef cattle and hogs. Others grow corn, hay, or oats. Many of these crops become animal feed.

In 2016, 1,279,000 dairy cows lived in Wisconsin.

CARR VALLEY CHEESE FACTORY IN LA VALLE

Hot vats of steamy milk. Lumpy curds and creamy whey. Then, at last, the finished product. Golden wheels of cheese! You're touring Carr Valley Cheese factory in La Valle. You can see every step of the cheese-making process. Of course, there's a treat at the end. You munch your heart out on free samples!

Got milk? Wisconsin does. Just think of all those cows. Much of their milk ends up as cheese. You'll find cheese factories all over the state.

Wisconsin also makes "hogs"! That's a nickname for motorcycles. Harley-Davidson motorcycles come from Wisconsin. Sorry, no free samples!

Taste some delicious cheese at Carr Valley Cheese factory!

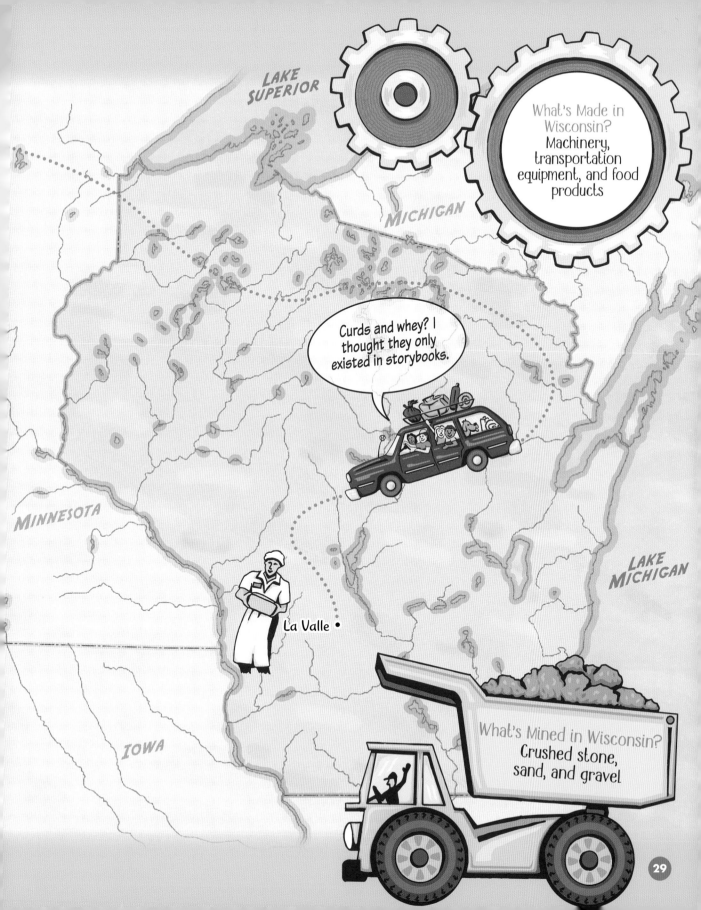

Aaron Rodgers is the Packers' star quarterback.

Hey, Mom, how about some Cheesehead earrings? How about a Cheesehead soap-on-a-rope?

Dear Mr. Lombardi:
The Packers were pretty lousy until you came along. You made them champs. No wonder the Super Bowl trophy was named after you!

Your fan,
Chee Z. Head

post card

Mr. Vince Lombardi
1913-1970
Green Bay, WI

Green Bay

LAKE MICHIGAN

MINNESOTA

IOWA

The Green Bay Packers won the Super Bowl in 1967, 1968, 1997, and 2011.

WISCONSIN SPORTS TEAMS
Green Bay Packers (football)
Milwaukee Brewers (baseball)
Milwaukee Bucks (basketball)

Milwaukee

Vince Lombardi coached the Packers from 1959 to 1967.

GREEN BAY'S CHEESEHEADS

I t looks like cheese. It's shaped like cheese. It's even got holes like Swiss cheese. But don't bite it! It's a Cheesehead hat!

Wisconsin loves its Green Bay Packers football team. Packers fans call themselves Cheeseheads. They wear big cheese-wedge hats. Cheeseheads are loyal fans. They pack Lambeau Field season after season.

Fans wear team jerseys and cheer on the Packers.

THE HOUSE ON THE ROCK IN SPRING GREEN

You're hanging out over the valley. Look down past your feet to the forest floor. It's more than 15 stories down! Suddenly everything begins to sway. Help!

You're in the House on the Rock in Spring Green. It's perched atop a rock tower. And you've walked into the Infinity Room. This long, pointy room sticks out in mid-air.

This whole house is full of strange things. Just check it out. Music machines with moving figures. More than 200 dollhouses. The world's largest carousel, with 269 carousel animals. Three giant organs, one with 15 keyboards. And a sea monster battling a giant octopus. Yikes!

See a wide variety of musical instruments at the House on the Rock.

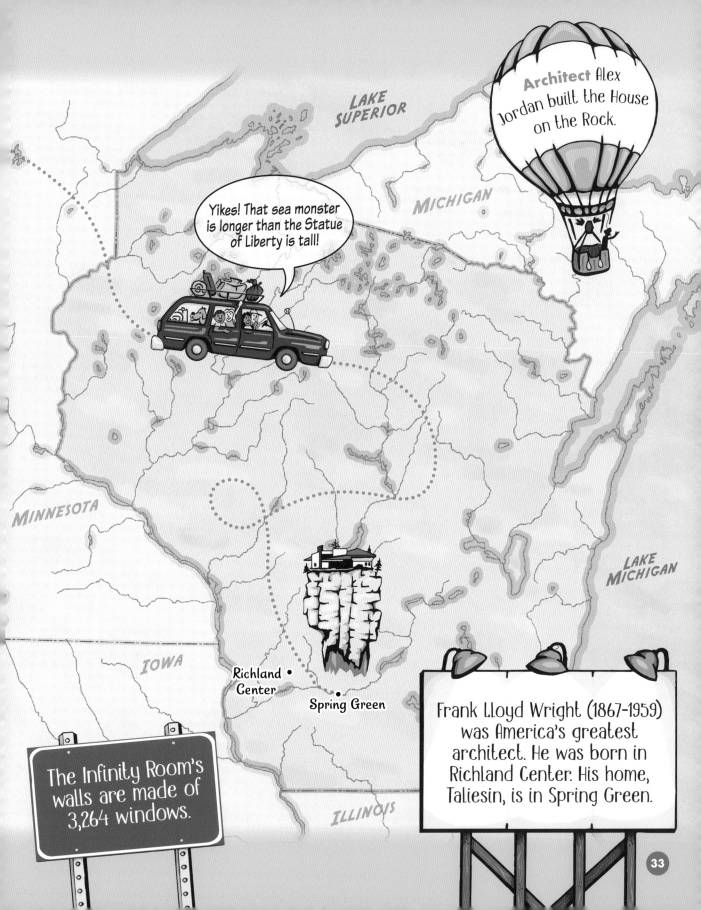

EAA AIRVENTURE IN OSHKOSH

You're soaring over Oshkosh. Your helicopter dips, swoops, and hovers. And way down there are thousands of aircraft.

You're at EAA AirVenture! It's a big summertime aircraft festival in Oshkosh. You'll see warplanes, seaplanes, and antique planes. Even planes that people built themselves. The air shows are awesome, too. Fearless **daredevils** do amazing stunts in the air.

While you're there, stroll over to Pioneer Airport. Then hop aboard for your helicopter ride!

Watch the U.S. Air Force Thunderbirds fly in formation at AirVenture.

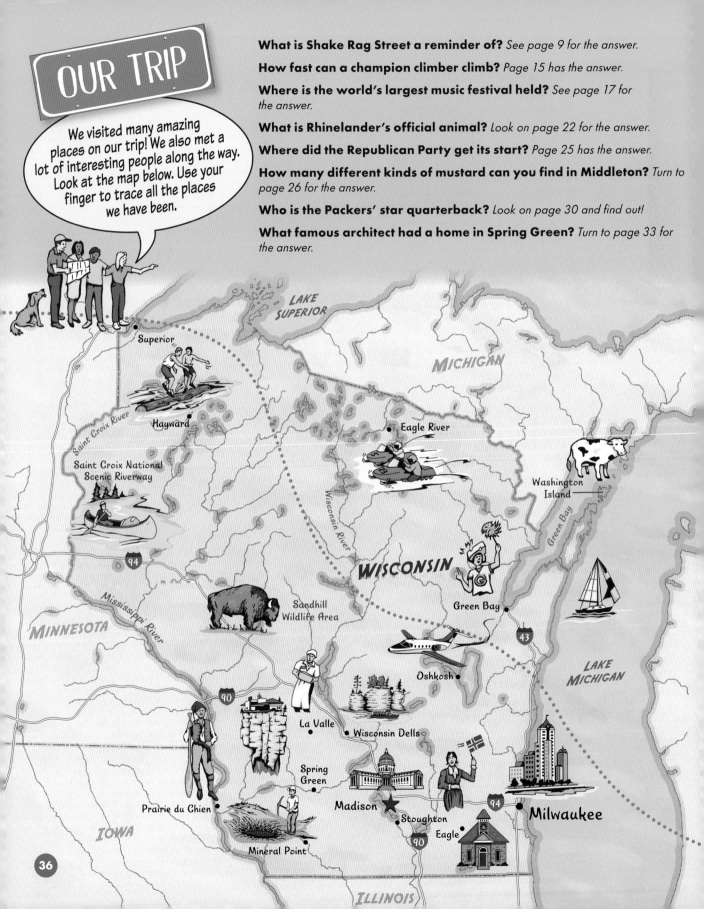

OUR TRIP

We visited many amazing places on our trip! We also met a lot of interesting people along the way. Look at the map below. Use your finger to trace all the places we have been.

What is Shake Rag Street a reminder of? *See page 9 for the answer.*

How fast can a champion climber climb? *Page 15 has the answer.*

Where is the world's largest music festival held? *See page 17 for the answer.*

What is Rhinelander's official animal? *Look on page 22 for the answer.*

Where did the Republican Party get its start? *Page 25 has the answer.*

How many different kinds of mustard can you find in Middleton? *Turn to page 26 for the answer.*

Who is the Packers' star quarterback? *Look on page 30 and find out!*

What famous architect had a home in Spring Green? *Turn to page 33 for the answer.*

LAKE SUPERIOR

MICHIGAN

Superior

Hayward

Saint Croix River

Saint Croix National Scenic Riverway

Eagle River

Washington Island

Green Bay

Wisconsin River

WISCONSIN

94

Mississippi River

MINNESOTA

Sandhill Wildlife Area

Green Bay

Oshkosh

43

LAKE MICHIGAN

90

La Valle

Wisconsin Dells

Spring Green

Madison

Milwaukee

Prairie du Chien

Stoughton

Eagle

94

90

IOWA

Mineral Point

ILLINOIS

State flag

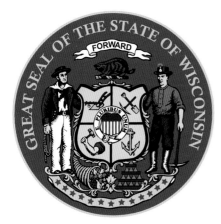

State seal

STATE SYMBOLS

State animal: Badger

State beverage: Milk

State bird: Robin

State dance: Polka

State dog: American water spaniel

State domesticated animal: Dairy cow

State fish: Muskellunge

State flower: Wood violet

State fossil: Trilobite

State grain: Corn

State insect: Honeybee

State mineral: Galena

State peace symbol: Mourning dove

State rock: Red granite

State soil: Antigo silt loam

State tree: Sugar maple

State wildlife animal: White-tailed deer

STATE SONG

"ON, WISCONSIN!"

Words by J. S. Hubbard and Charles D. Rosa, music by William T. Purdy

On, Wisconsin!
On, Wisconsin!
Grand old badger state!
We, thy loyal sons and daughters,
Hail thee, good and great.
On, Wisconsin!
On, Wisconsin!
Champion of the right,
"Forward," our motto—
God will give thee might!

That was a great trip! We have traveled all over Wisconsin! There are a few places that we didn't have time for, though. Next time, we'll stop by Saint Croix National Scenic Riverway in Saint Croix Falls. People who visit canoe, hike, or fish. If they're lucky, they sometimes spot eagles, wolves, or deer!

FAMOUS PEOPLE

Butler, Caron (1980–), basketball player

Catt, Carrie (1859–1947), women's rights activist

Harris, Devin (1983–), basketball player

Houdini, Harry (1874–1926), magician

Kaepernick, Colin (1987–), football player

Kessel, Phil (1987–), hockey player

La Follette, Robert (1855–1925), governor and senator

Lombardi, Vince (1913–1970), football coach

Meir, Golda (1898–1978), prime minister of Israel

Muir, John (1838–1914), naturalist, conservationist

O'Keeffe, Georgia (1887–1986), artist

Patrick, Danica (1982–), race car driver

Rehnquist, William (1924–2005), Supreme Court chief justice

Ruffalo, Mark (1967–), actor

Ryan, Paul (1970–), politician

Suter, Ryan (1985–), hockey player

Thomas, Joe (1984–), football player

Watt, JJ (1989–), football player

Welles, Orson (1915–1985), film director, actor

Wilder, Laura Ingalls (1867–1957), author

Wright, Frank Lloyd (1867–1959), architect

Zimmermann, Jordan (1986–), baseball player

WORDS TO KNOW

architect (AR-ki-tekt) a person who designs buildings

breweries (BROO-ur-eez) places where beer is made

dairy (DAIR-ee) having to do with milk and milk products

daredevils (DAIR-dev-ilz) people who perform dangerous acts

ethnic (ETH-nik) having to do with a person's race or nationality

immigrants (IM-uh-gruhnts) people who leave their home country for another country

industry (IN-duh-stree) a type of business

legislature (LEJ-iss-lay-chur) a group of people who make laws for a state or country

lumberjacks (LUHM-bur-jaks) workers who cut down forest trees and transport them

peninsula (puh-NIN-suh-luh) a piece of land almost completely surrounded by water

tomahawk (TOM-uh-hawk) a Native American ax

troll (TROHL) a creepy creature in the folklore of Norway, Sweden, and Denmark

TO LEARN MORE

IN THE LIBRARY

Howell, Brian. *Green Bay Packers.* Mankato, MN: The Child's World, 2016.

Pferdehirt, Julia. *Freedom Train North: Stories of the Underground Railroad in Wisconsin.* Madison, WI: Wisconsin Historical Society, 2011.

Rechner, Amy. *Wisconsin.* Minneapolis, MN: Bellwether Media, 2014.

ON THE WEB

Visit our Web site for links about Wisconsin:
childsworld.com/links

Note to Parents, Teachers, and Librarians: We routinely verify our Web links to make sure they are safe and active sites. So encourage your readers to check them out!

PLACES TO VISIT OR CONTACT

Travel Wisconsin
travelwisconsin.com
201 West Washington Avenue
Madison, WI 53703
800/432-8747
For more information about traveling in Wisconsin

Wisconsin Historical Museum
historicalmuseum.wisconsinhistory.org
30 N. Carroll Street
Madison, WI 53703
608/264-6555
For more information about the history of Wisconsin

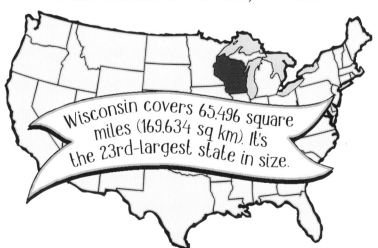

Wisconsin covers 65,496 square miles (169,634 sq km). It's the 23rd-largest state in size.

INDEX

Bye, Badger State.
We had a great time.
We'll come back soon!